One snowy Christmas, Darling received a very special gift from her husband. She unwrapped the brightly wrapped box, and out popped a beautiful little puppy! "Oh, Jim Dear, she's beautiful! I think I'll call her Lady."

Lady had found a very happy home with Darling and Jim Dear. Her afternoons were spent playing in the park with Darling. And later she would race Jim Dear home from work.

One summer day, Jim Dear came home with a surprise for Lady. "Here you are, girl—your very own collar and license. Why don't you show them off to Jock and Trusty?"

Lady trotted proudly next door to see the neighboring dogs. "Notice anything different, Trusty?"

"Why, Miss Lady," drawled the aging bloodhound. "You've got a new collar."

Jock, the Scottie, added, "Aye, and it looks very expensive."

Later that summer, Lady noticed a change in Jim Dear and Darling. The races home stopped, as did the afternoon walks. Instead, Darling just sat home and knitted. Poor lonely Lady sat outside and wondered why her owners were acting so strangely.

The answer came a few weeks later. There was tremendous excitement in the house. Jim Dear happily telephoned his Aunt Sarah. "It's here! And it's a baby... a boy! I'm a daddy!"

Lady tiptoed upstairs and peeked carefully into a frilly crib. "Oh, it's the cutest little human I've ever seen! So this is why Jim Dear and Darling were acting so strangely!"

Lady rushed outside to tell Jock and Trusty about the beautiful baby. As she talked, a stray dog with no collar or license entered the yard. He sauntered right up to Lady. "Hello, Pigeon. I couldn't help overhearing your conversation, and I think you're all wrong. Why, babies are just cute little bundles of trouble!"

Jock had heard about this intruder. His name was Tramp, and he always managed to escape the dogcatcher's net. Jock didn't like him. "Off with you now, you mongrel!"

When Jim Dear and Darling left for a weekend, Aunt
Sarah came to stay with the baby. And much to Lady's
dismay, Aunt Sarah had brought along her two Siamese
cats!

They were troublemakers from the start. One cat
headed right for the canary cage, while the other tried
to make a meal out of the goldfish! Lady chased after

them and spoiled their plans, but not before the cats had made a shambles of the living room. Aunt Sarah came running! "Merciful heavens, look at this mess!"

The two pesky cats pretended to be hurt. Aunt Sarah cuddled them. "Did that wicked dog attack you, my innocent little angels? Well, I know how to take care of that ruffian!"

Aunt Sarah didn't waste a moment. She grabbed Lady and marched right down to the local pet shop. "Clerk, I want a muzzle. A good strong one!"

The shopkeeper strapped a heavy muzzle onto Lady's face. It was so tight that she could hardly open her mouth!

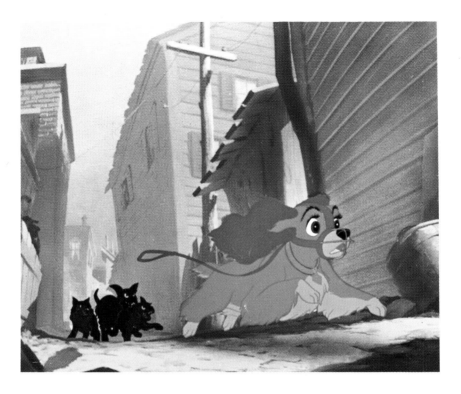

Lady wiggled out of Aunt Sarah's arms and bolted out of the store in fear. Up one street and down another she fled, trying to escape the horrible muzzle. She soon found herself lost—and in a very bad part of town. Three big dogs spotted Lady and gave chase, snarling and snapping, until they had her trapped in a blind alley!

As the snarling dogs inched closer to Lady, another
dog leaped to her rescue. It was Tramp! Singlehandedly,
he fought the vicious dogs and sent them yelping away!
Then he turned to Lady. "Hey, Pidge, what are you
doing on this side of the tracks? I thought you—huh? A
muzzle? Aw, you poor kid! We've got to get that thing
off. Come on."

Tramp led Lady to the City Zoo. At a pond, they found a beaver struggling to pull a heavy log into the water. "Pardon me, friend. It looks like you need a log puller. I happen to have a handy-dandy one here, modeled by the little lady. Just nip it off, and it's yours!"

The beaver quickly nibbled through a strap, and Lady was free of the hated muzzle.

"Come on, Pidge, let's find a place to celebrate!"
Tramp seemed to be known and welcomed everywhere
they went. He had a different place to eat every day of
the week. "It's Wednesday, Pidge. That means we go to
Tony's Restaurant. You'll love it!"

Tony had a plate of bones all ready, but when he saw that Tramp had brought a lady friend, he served them a delicious dinner of spaghetti and meatballs! Then Tony took out his accordion and sang a beautiful love song, while Lady and Tramp dined by candlelight! Lady marveled at Tramp's carefree life — so different from her own.

After the romantic dinner, Lady and Tramp walked through the park to the top of a hill overlooking the city. "Look down there, Pigeon. There's a great, big world out there with no fence around it, where two dogs like us could find adventure and excitement!"

"It sounds wonderful, Tramp, but who would watch over Jim Dear, Darling and the baby?"

"You win, Pidge. I guess we're just too different."

   As he escorted Lady home, Tramp noticed some hens
sleeping in a yard. "Hey, let's wake up those fat, lazy
biddies!"
   "But won't we hurt them, Tramp?"
   "Naw, we'll just stir them up a bit. It'll be fun!"
Tramp raced into the yard, barking wildly. Chickens
went fluttering and squawking about until the owner
rushed outside with his shotgun! "That's the signal to
get out of here, Pidge!"

Lady tried to keep up with Tramp as he darted around corners and scrambled over fences, but soon she was lost again. Without warning, the city dogcatcher pounced on poor Lady and carted her off to the dog pound! "That Tramp—I never would have guessed he was the type to desert a lady!"

Lady had never been so scared and humiliated in all her life! The dingy pound was full of sad, scruffy dogs who stared longingly at her license. They told her that it was her ticket out of there and wished they all had one, too.

Soon Aunt Sarah arrived to take Lady home. But as punishment for running away, she chained her to the doghouse. Poor Lady was feeling lonely and sad when Tramp came trotting into the yard. "Hi, Pidge! I heard what happened. I came over to tell you how sorry I am."

"You ran out on me, and I took the blame. It was so embarrassing! I never want to see you again! Goodbye!"

As Tramp hung his head and turned to leave, Lady
spied a big, ugly rat climbing into the baby's window!
She tugged on her chain and desperately called for help.
"Tramp, hurry! There's a rat in the baby's room!"

Tramp raced into the house and up the stairs, and
burst into the baby's room. The rat was creeping toward
the baby's crib. Tramp pounced on the rat and killed it.

The noise from Tramp's fight awakened Aunt Sarah. She rushed into the baby's room. "Oh, you vicious brute! Trying to attack the baby!" Aunt Sarah hadn't even seen the rat! She forced Tramp into a closet and locked the door. "Now I'll call the dogcatcher and have that brute taken away!"

Jock and Trusty watched as Tramp was locked in the dogcatcher's wagon. "Well, Trusty, there he goes, off to the pound. I was certain he was no good the moment I first laid eyes on him."

"Yeah, but I never thought he'd attack a helpless baby!"

Just then, Jim Dear and Darling returned home. Lady gave a desperate tug and broke her chain. She ran into the house, barking frantically at Jim Dear. "Look, Darling. Lady's trying to tell us something. What is it, girl?"

Lady raced upstairs to the baby's room to show Jim Dear the truth. "Oh, my goodness! Darling, come here!"

"What is it, Jim? Oh—a rat!"

"That means that Tramp is actually innocent. He saved the baby! But now he's being taken to the dog pound to be destroyed!"

When Jock overheard this, he felt ashamed. "Trusty, we've misjudged Tramp badly. We've got to rescue him!" The two dogs raced after the dogcatcher's wagon, barking fiercely. The frightened horses bolted, the wagon overturned, and the door sprang open. Tramp was free!

Jim Dear and Darling were so grateful to Tramp that they bought him a collar and license. Now he was part of the family! The next Christmas, Lady and Tramp celebrated with their own family—four adorable puppies!